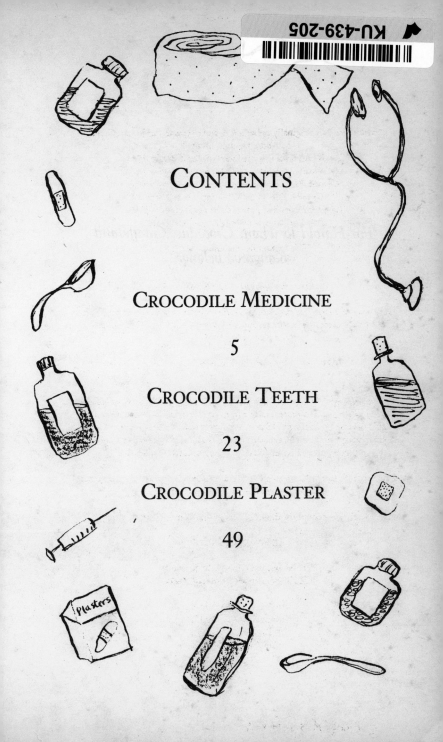

CONTENTS

Plasters

*For Harold to whom Crocodile, Giraffe and
Kangaroo belong.*

CROCODILE MEDICINE

CHAPTER ONE

Once upon a time, there was an extremely large hospital. It had hundreds of windows, a great many rooms, row after row of beds, and a large notice outside saying CITY HOSPITAL – QUIET PLEASE!

In this hospital was a little girl called Julie.

She had come there to get better, because she wasn't feeling very well.

Next door to the hospital lived three friends, Giraffe, Kangaroo and Crocodile.

Kangaroo did the cooking, Giraffe did the shopping, and Crocodile was meant to do the housework. But mostly he stayed in bed. He said he had a pain, but nobody believed him.

Julie had been in the hospital for quite a long time. She had a bed, a cupboard next to it where she kept her toothbrush and flannel and things like that, a teddybear, and lots and lots of other children all around.

There was Tony. Sister said he was a pickle. He teased the nurses and called them rude names. He was always in trouble.

Then there was Isabelle. She woke up in the night and cried. But in the daytime she was quite happy.

Alan was in the bed next to Julie. He had a very bad pain when he came into hospital. But now he was a bit better. He had ice cream every day for dinner. But he still had to stay in bed.

Most days somebody new came,
and sometimes people went home. Julie
wished she could leave too. She didn't
like being left behind when other
children went home.

There were several different kinds
of nurses looking after Julie and the other
children. Thin ones, fat ones, tall ones,
pink ones, brown ones. They all wore
different clothes, in different colours.

Julie had a favourite nurse called Nurse Rachel.

In the morning the Doctors would walk through the room where Julie was, and talk to the children, and listen to their chests. Julie liked Doctor Chumley best.

Sometimes Julie played. Sometimes she talked to the other children. Sometimes she had to take medicine. Sometimes she went along the passage with Nurse Rachel to look through the glass at the tiny babies, or into the children's kitchen to see if they were cooking something nice.

Or into Sister's room at coffee time. Sometimes she slept in her bed, because she didn't feel very well. And sometimes she was bored bored bored, and wished she could come out of hospital and never see it again.

CHAPTER TWO

One day she was looking out of the window wishing she was at home, when she saw a face looking straight at her.

"Hello!" Julie said, "who are you?"

"Giraffe," the face said. "I live next door. I've just been shopping. Why are all those people in bed?"

"They have all got pains," Julie said. "They come here to get better."

"Oh!" Giraffe smiled.
"Can I bring my friend?
He says he's got a pain"
"I expect so. Just a
minute, I'll ask nurse."
Julie went to fetch her
favourite nurse.

"Nurse! Nurse!" she called, "Come
quickly."

But Nurse Rachel was nowhere to
be found, and everyone else was busy.
When at last Julie and her favourite nurse
got back to the window, the face had
gone.

Some time later, Julie was still looking out of the window hoping to see Giraffe again, when she heard a lot of noise behind her.

"Oh dear! Oh dear! Oh! Oh! I've got a pain!" and there was Crocodile holding his tummy and groaning.

"You'd better get into bed," Julie said, "if you've got a pain. I'll tell Nurse."

So Crocodile got into bed, and Nurse came to look at him. "Hello," she said, "you look a bit unhappy, don't you? I'll get Staff Nurse."

So Staff Nurse came and took his temperature. "Mm," she said, "I'll get Sister."

Sister came. "Dear dear dear! You poor old chap. Have you got a pain?"

Crocodile opened his mouth very wide.

"Oh!" Sister said. "What a lot of teeth! I'll get Doctor."

So Doctor Chumley came and sat by the bed. "Now," he said, "where's this pain?"

Crocodile looked more and more miserable.

"I don't know!"

"Is it in your tummy?"

"I don't think so."

"Is it in your legs?"

"No."

"Is it in your arms?"

"No."

Crocodile shook his big green head, and then, suddenly opened his mouth very wide indeed. "It's inside here!" he said.

Dr Chumley looked as if he didn't much like the sight of all those teeth.

"Mm," he said. "It's very dark down there. Can someone fetch me a torch?"

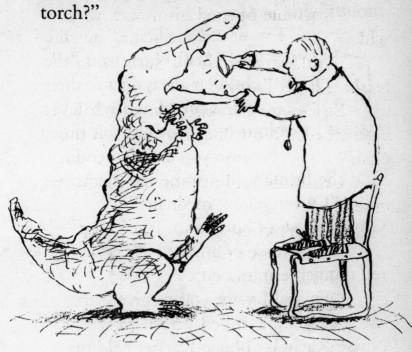

"Ah yes!" Dr Chumley said when he had peered down Crocodile's throat. "It's very sore right the way down into your tummy. No wonder you've got a pain. I'll give you some medicine."

So Staff Nurse brought some green medicine.

"Here you are dear," she said. "Just drink this down." Crocodile shut his mouth with a snap.

 "I want red medicine," he said. "Well," Staff Nurse said, "the children always drink their medicine down whatever colour it is. But just this time; because you are a crocodile." And she brought him some red medicine.

"I want yellow medicine!" Crocodile said, "but I want it in a cup."

Staff Nurse poured the red medicine into a cup.

"Er, and I want you to give it to me." Crocodile smiled very hard at Nurse Rachel. Nurse Rachel held the cup in her hand. "I'm afraid of all those teeth!" she said after a moment.

"So am I!" Dr Chumley and Sister and Staff Nurse said all together.

"I'm not!" laughed Julie. "I'll give it to him," and Crocodile swallowed down every little drop.

16

CHAPTER THREE

In the morning Crocodile felt a bit better, but he still had a pain. So Julie told him a story about Goldilocks and the three bears, and he went to sleep.

"You are good," Julie said, stroking his head.

Just before dinner Staff Nurse came to see him. "I'm going to give you a little scratch," she said to Crocodile. "It's to help take your pain away."

Crocodile began to look unhappy again.

"What's that, a scratch?" he asked.

"Only an injection," Julie said.

Crocodile looked even more unhappy.

"I don't like injections," he said.

Staff Nurse put her hand on his head.

"You'll hardly feel it," she said, "just a little prick and it's all finished. Then you can have your dinner."

"I don't want any dinner."

Julie held his hand. "Oh it's a lovely dinner today. And you'll have ice cream I expect. But only if you have your injection first."

Crocodile made a terrible fuss. He roared and yelled, twisted and turned, and pulled up all the bed clothes over his head. But his tail was still sticking out, so that's where Staff Nurse gave him his injection, in his tail! And I don't think he felt it at all.

"Come out, Crocodile," Julie said.
"It's all over. Dinner time now. Look, the
trolley is here!"

Crocodile poked his head out from
under the bed clothes. "What about the
injection?" he said.

Julie laughed. "It's over, finished.
Dinner time now."

The ice cream was delicious. Julie and Crocodile had second helpings.

In the afternoon, Crocodile's friends came to visit him. I'm afraid they were rather a nuisance.

Kangaroo kept jumping everywhere and knocking things over. And Giraffe was really much too tall. Sister said it made her neck ache to talk to him. But Julie liked them, because they told her funny stories, and made her laugh.

In the evening the Doctor came in. "And how are you?" he said to Crocodile.

"I've still got a pain," Crocodile said, "just a very small one."

"Yes, I expect you have. Well, you can't go home yet. We want you quite better."

"Oh good!" Crocodile said. "This bed is more comfortable than the one at home. Shall I have some more medicine?"

"I'll give it to him," Julie said, and this time she gave him a very sticky orange medicine through a straw.

Crocodile dribbled it all down his front and on the blankets.

"What a mess you are making," Julie said, giggling.

And that's all I can tell you for the moment. Crocodile is still there, and so is Julie. Kangaroo and Giraffe come to visit them quite often. Sister says she doesn't know whether to laugh or cry when she sees them arrive.

Crocodile eats his dinner and does jigsaw puzzles. He doesn't make such a fuss about his injections now, and he likes his nice comfortable bed. But of course the best thing of all is that he has Julie next to him. I expect she is talking to him at this very moment.

CROCODILE
TEETH

CHAPTER ONE

Julie lay in her bed having a rest after
dinner. In the afternoon she was going
to have a party, even though she was in
hospital.

She should have been very excited
and happy. Today was her birthday. Tony
was coming to the party (easy, he was in
the next bed). So was Nurse Rachel and
Staff Nurse; Isabelle in her wheelchair,
Danny, Thomas, Dawn, Jeanie, Ahmed

and baby John. Even Dr Chumley was going to look in, Sister said.

"Time to get up, Julie." Staff nurse hurried past. "Your party will be starting soon."

Julie stayed where she was. Sister walked by with somebody's mother.

"How's the birthday girl?" Sister said smiling. "You look sleepy."

I wish I was at home, thought Julie, and shut her eyes.

"Wake up, Julie!" This time it was Nurse Rachel. "We'll soon be having tea."

"I don't want any tea . . ."

"On your birthday? Of course you do. Now, red jersey or something special? Pink dress, green trousers?"

"Red jersey," Julie said.

It was definitely a special tea, and Tony gave her a present: a small brown snail in a matchbox.

CHAPTER TWO

The long table was big enough for everyone, and covered with delicious things: honey sandwiches, egg sandwiches, chocolate wafers, red and orange jellies, fruit juice and straws in paper mugs.

"Hmm!" said Staff nurse bringing another chair. "Everyone's teeth will need a good clean after all this! I can't imagine what the kitchen is thinking of, it's nothing but sugar!"

They had just sat down and Julie
was wondering whether Snail would like
a sandwich or a drink first, when
somebody walked in through the door,
a visitor.

"Ah !" said Nurse Rachel, "A
birthday surprise for you, Julie. Here's
Crocodile!"

Suddenly, Julie felt very happy.

"It's my birthday today," she said at
once to Crocodile. "I am quite old now,

you know, so Snail and I are having a party." She pulled out a stool. "Sit next to me, and you can help me cut my cake."

Julie was so very pleased to see her old friend, she hardly noticed the strip of bandage wound round and round his head.

Crocodile sat down slowly, groaning and sighing.

"Oh dear!" Julie said looking at him more carefully. "Is there? Are you?"

Crocodile looked more and more miserable. Tears began to trickle down his long knobbly green face.

"Don't tell me you're ill again?" said Nurse Rachel handing round the sandwiches. "Too ill for ice cream? What's the matter this time?"

Crocodile shook his head sadly. "Not very well I'm afraid," he whispered.

"It's my head, my face actually. I've got this terrible pain. Even my nose hurts."

"Ready for your cake, Julie?" asked Staff Nurse. She lit the candles, picked up the cake and carried it to the table.

"Don't forget to wish when you blow out the candles," she said.

It was a beautiful cake; pink, with sugar decorations, coloured sugar buttons round the sides, and just the right number of candles.

"Oh!" Crocodile gazed at the cake his face brightening a little. "Birthday cake!"

"Would you like some?" Julie asked.

"Well, it's not that I'm ill exactly . . . I mean . . . cake would probably do me good . . . I expect . . ."

"Of course it would," Julie was laughing. Crocodile began to smile through his tears.

"Probably birthday cake is just what I need," he said, watching Staff Nurse cutting slices. But Julie had only taken a couple of bites when a fearful noise started beside her: Crocodile rolling about on the floor groaning and weeping.

"OH! OH!" he cried, "Oh dear! The pain. Oh! Ohhhh! . . ." and so on.

"I think he's got a pain," Julie said to Snail who was creeping very slowly round and round the edge of her plate. "Or one of those candles was still alight."

At that moment Sister and Dr Chumley came in.

"Happy birthday, Julie!" Sister said smiling. "Oh! There's that Crocodile. Has he come to the party? What's he doing down there?"

"Got a pain," Julie said, "I think."

"OHHHH!" roared Crocodile, squirming about on the floor, "My face, my poor face. What shall I do? . . . Oh! Oh dear!"

"You do look a bit poorly," Dr Chumley said kneeling down beside him. "Where's this pain, then?"

"HERE!" bellowed Crocodile rolling his eyes and pointing to his face.

"Inside or outside, your head?"

"Ohhh!"

Julie stroked poor Crocodile very very gently on his back. "Let Doctor have a look," she said.

What a sight when finally the bandage came off. One side of Crocodile's face was swollen up like a football. He opened his huge mouth and pointed. "In here, at the bottom."

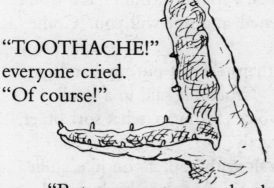

"TOOTHACHE!" everyone cried. "Of course!"

"But you must go to the dentist at once," Dr Chumley said, "at once."

"I have," sobbed Crocodile, "but they are all frightened of me. Imagine, of me! They say, 'too many sharp teeth', and run."

"Never heard of a dentist running away," this was Tony, "it's generally . . ."

"Be quiet!" Nurse Rachel said.

Dr Chumley looked at Crocodile for a moment.

"Well, we must get your pain taken away; can't have you walking about in that state, and on Julie's birthday too." He stood up. "We'd better get you looked at. There's a very good dentist in this hospital, a friend of mine. He won't be frightened, and nor will you. Come along."

"Perhaps I'll just put my bandage on again," Crocodile said in a small worried voice. "I mean, what sort of, er, dentist exactly?"

"I'll sit with you, if you like," Julie said, putting Snail back in his box and helping herself to another piece of cake, "to cheer you up."

CHAPTER THREE

It was just as well Julie went with him. Mr Brown, the dentist, may not have been frightened of Crocodile, but poor Crocodile was terribly scared of him. Of everything in the room.

"What's that? What are those? That's a funny smell?" he whispered, staring at the rows of silvery gleaming dentist things on Mr Brown's tray. "And that NOISE?"

"This," Mr Brown picked up one of the shiny metal instruments, "has got a mirror on the end of it, so I can see the back of your teeth. Show him Julie. That lovely smell," Mr Brown sniffed the air, "is oil of cloves. And disinfectant – in the pink glass there. The noise is my special sort of mouth vacuum cleaner for . . ."

"Does it hurt?" Crocodile asked immediately.

"Oh no, just sucks out the water and the bits. Here is my water drill – my air and water drill. Makes a sort of whistling noise. And this," Mr Brown smiled at Crocodile, " – is my chair." He pressed a button on the floor. "I can make it go up . . . or . . . down. Like to show him Julie?"

"Just a minute," Julie said, "I'm looking for Snail. He's gone for a walk, and I don't want him squashed."

When she found Snail, Julie climbed into Mr Brown's chair. "Up!" she called. The chair rose slowly toward the ceiling, higher and higher, nearly as tall as Mr Brown himself. Julie giggled. "Down, please," she said. And down she went until she was nearly sitting on Mr Brown's feet.

"Want to try?" Mr Brown asked Crocodile.

"It, you, won't do anything? I mean . . ."

"Certainly not." Mr Brown smiled. "I'll tell you - about anything I want to do."

After Crocodile had gone up in the chair, down in the chair, halfway up, three-quarters down fourteen times or so, had been told almost as many times what everything was, what it was for, how it worked, Mr Brown said, "Now! What about this toothache, then?"

Crocodile closed his eyes. "It's very bad, I'm afraid."

"Where is it exactly? The pain?"

"Here!" Crocodile opened his enormous mouth. Mr Brown didn't seem particulary alarmed at the sight of all those very sharp teeth; just gave him a pair of dark glasses so that his pale Crocodile eyes wouldn't be dazzled, switched on an extremely bright light and had a look.

"Open your mouth *very* wide-," Mr Brown peered and poked, and had another look all around the inside of Crocodile's mouth with his little mirror. "Dear me!" he said, shaking his head.

Bang! Crocodile shut his mouth with a snap. Fortunately only the mirror was between his teeth.

"If you do that," Mr Brown said, "I can't see anything. And you will break my mirror."

"Ohhhh!" groaned Crocodile opening his mouth again. "Sorry. It does hurt so. It's the worse pain I have ever had, I think . . ."

Tears began to trickle off his nose.

Mr Brown turned off his bright overhead light and sat down beside Crocodile.

"Like me to take it away?" he said. "The pain? You've got a horrible rotten old tooth at the back there. No wonder it's hurting so much. I'd better take it out."

"Out? My teeth?" Crocodile began to scramble from the chair.

"Just the bad one. The others I can mend quite easily ."

"Others?" Crocodile stared at him, "What others?"

"Two at the bottom, three at the top. All got holes," Mr Brown said cheerfully. "But I can mend them. No problem."

Crocodile leaned back in the chair, the tears running down his face and onto his chin.

"No more pain if that tooth comes out," Mr Brown said.

"Er how? How, does it . . . ?"

"An injection first–"

"Where? I don't like . . ."

"Up near the tooth–"

"IN MY MOUTH?"

"That's the nasty bit, but only for a moment. Then we wait for a few minutes, until everything goes numb–"

"Numb?"

"-on that side of your mouth. So you don't feel anything, and one, two, three – out it comes!"

Crocodile lay in Mr Brown's chair holding his poor aching swollen face thinking. "Completely gone?" he said at last, "The pain? Just one tooth?"

Mr Brown nodded. "Just one. I promise."

Silence.

Julie watched Snail creeping along her finger.

"It only takes a moment," she said, "really."

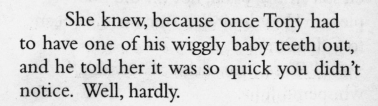

She knew, because once Tony had to have one of his wiggly baby teeth out, and he told her it was so quick you didn't notice. Well, hardly.

Crocodile opened his mouth slowly, shut it, opened it again just a little.

"Right," Mr Brown switched on the light again, "here we go, then. But no more shutting your mouth suddenly, wide open all the time, please. Hold up your arm, leg, if there's anything you don't like, and I'll stop."

You couldn't exactly say that Crocodile didn't notice anything, but it wasn't too bad; and Mr Brown was very kind and gentle. Quick too. Julie watched. And the tooth, well! Black and crumbling, a great mouldy hole in the middle and quite worn away on one side.

"That's better!" Mr Brown smiled at Crocodile. "No wonder you had toothache. Like to rinse your mouth out a bit? The pink glass beside you, and - er, spit in the basin, not on the floor please. How long is it since you've been to a dentist?"

"*Rinse* - not drink, Crocodile," whispered Julie.

"He's never been much, ever, I think – have you?"

Crocodile shook his head mournfully and blew bubbles into the pink glass through his nose.

"Well, you will get toothache again if your other teeth aren't mended." Mr Brown sounded very sure. "I'll start now, shall I?"

"Er . . . how?"

"Take out the bad bits with my water-machine – Whistling Willie I call him, and fill up the holes. Good as new."

"I don't think I feel quite well enough yet."

"You'll feel a lot worse if those holes aren't mended," Mr Brown said. "Don't chew my vacuum cleaner pipe, please, or the water won't run away. Let's start, shall we? Put your dark glasses on, they suit you. And open your mouth very wide. I'm going to shine my light . . ."

Crocodile's face and inside his mouth were still numb from the injection; so although he heard a lot of noise, whistling, water gurgling, he didn't feel a thing – except a kind of buzzing.

"That's the drill," Julie said, "taking

out the bad bits. And that creaking scrunching sound is filling up the holes to mend them."

"Aagh . . . !" Crocodile said, his mouth wide open.

Mr Brown got rather wet, but he didn't seem to mind too much. "Very very good," he said, "but that's enough for today. Come back on Friday and we'll finish them off."

Crocodile felt a bit wobbly when he got down from the chair.

CHAPTER FOUR

"My legs have turned to string," he told Nurse Rachel when he was back on the ward.

"They look alright to me," she said. But as he had had a tooth out she let him lie down on one of the empty beds; and Julie told him a story about the Three Bears going to the dentist.

"He's asleep," Julie said to Snail when bedtime came, and Nurse Rachel was folding up her clothes.

"Better leave him, then," Nurse
Rachel smiled, "with his string legs. See
how he is in the morning,"

Crocodile slept all night, and all
through breakfast, surprisingly, as Tony,
Snail and a friend had built a garage
under his bed.

"How's your tooth today?" Julie
asked when he woke up at last.

"Tooth. Oh . . . !" Crocodile sat up and felt his face. "It's a bit sore, but the pain . . . has . . . it's better! Gone! So's the tooth," Crocodile added, "there's a space."

"You are brave," Julie said. "Can Snail have a look?"

"Oh hello, are you still here?" Nurse Rachel came in with the medicines. "Yes, I suppose you would be. Actually you are staying a few days, I think. Mr Brown wants to make sure your teeth are mended before you leave us."

"Can I have a party?" Crocodile said at once. "It's my birthday tomorrow."

"Is it now!" Nurse Rachel winked at Julie.

"And how old would you be?"

Crocodile thought hard. "About a hundred?"

"That's a lot of candles," Julie said laughing. "I'd better help you blow them out."

Everyone came to Crocodile's party, even Snail.

"He hasn't any teeth, has he, poor thing?" Crocodile said.

"Can't very well have ice cream, or cake, do you think?"

So they had a cabbage leaf for Snail, and water-cress and egg sandwiches, Crocodile's favourite; chocolate wafers, ice cream and a cake with so many candles on it that Julie couldn't count them. After he had made a birthday wish, everyone helped Crocodile blow out the candles. Then he told them what he wished; a birthday party every day.

"No chance!" Julie said giggling. "You should have kept it a secret."

Sister gave Crocodile a present. A large red toothbrush suitable for a very large mouth full of beautiful clean mended teeth. Crocodile teeth, she said.

CROCODILE
PLASTER

CHAPTER ONE

It was raining. Julie stared at the rain
trickling down the outside of the
hospital window. She was bored. Isabelle
was doing her lessons, Alan was asleep,
and her friend Crocodile had gone home
a long time ago. There was nobody to talk
to, nobody she wanted to talk to, that is.

Dr Chumley walked by.

"Hello, Julie," he said, "I like your
jersey!"

"I hate it," Julie said.

Staff Nurse hurried past carrying a tray full of medicines and pills. "Soon be tea-time, Julie," she said over her shoulder.

"I don't want any tea."

Then the Play Lady sat down. "Like to do some painting, Julie?" She had a trolley loaded with different coloured paints.

Julie looked at her crossly. "I HATE painting," she said. And she was just going to shout out something extremely rude about hospital, doctors, nurses, painting and everything else, when out of the corner of her eye she noticed something happening out in the courtyard in front of the hospital. Something interesting. The ambulance men were trying to get someone out of the ambulance – someone who wasn't exactly helping. First some red blankets came flying out through the doors; two pillows followed, then a box of bandages.

"Hmm," Julie smiled. "How naughty!"

"Tea-time, Julie!" Nurse Rachel called.

"Look!" Julie said, "SOMEONE is coming into hospital!"

She watched the ambulance men push a large bundle all wrapped up in blankets, out on a trolley.

"I can see a TAIL sticking out," Julie said. "I think it's Crocodile come back!"

But Nurse Rachel was busy doling out sandwiches and didn't hear her. Suddenly Julie felt very happy.

CHAPTER TWO

S he had nearly finished her tea, when
Crocodile was pushed into the room
in a wheel-chair.

He looked very sorry for himself.

"Whatever's the matter with you?"

"I've got a pain," said Crocodile.
"I think!"

"Well, you'd better get into bed
then," said Julie. "I'll tell Nurse."

"Oh my goodness! You're back!"

Nurse Rachel said as soon as she saw Crocodile. "What's the matter this time?"

"I've got a pain," Crocodile said. "Actually my legs are broken – I think. I fell out of bed, and then – I had an accident!"

"Oh dear! You don't look very comfortable anyway; your bandages are slipping. I'll go and tell Staff Nurse."

"Mmm," Staff Nurse said when she saw all the bandages, "broken legs! You seem to be walking alright. I'll fetch Sister."

Sister smiled when she saw Crocodile and all his bandages.

"Well!" she said, "What have you been doing? An accident? Doctor had better see you. Where exactly is your pain?"

But Crocodile just looked at her with tears in his eyes, and didn't say anything. Sister nodded her head. "I'll tell Doctor. He'll come and see you quite soon."

Crocodile watched Julie finishing her piece of cake.

"I think I *could* manage a little tea," he whispered. So he had four tomato and egg sandwiches, eight pieces of bread and butter, two chocolate biscuits, and two slices of fruit cake.

"You aren't very ill, are you? In spite of your broken legs?" Julie said.

When the tea-trolley had been cleared away, Doctor Chumley came in.

"Now," he said, sitting down by Crocodile's bed, "Where is this pain?"

Crocodile looked unhappy, and held up first one bandaged leg, and then the other. "I think they are all broken," he said. Doctor Chumley unwrapped the bandages, and felt Crocodile's legs gently all over. "They don't seem very broken to me," he said. "What about your head? Did you bang it?"

Crocodile thought for a moment. "I might have. Yes - it feels banged. I think I did."

"Well, let's see," Doctor Chumley said. "Er, shut your mouth please, and I'll take this bandage off too."

He looked at Crocodile's head very carefully. At his eyes, into his nose, down his throat. Then he listened to his chest and his back, and felt his tummy.

"That all seems fine," he said, "but you must have an X-ray. I'll tell Sister."

"What's an X-ray?" Crocodile asked Julie unhappily.

"Just a machine that takes photographs of your bones," Julie said. "It doesn't hurt. I've had some of my bones done. Will you help me with my painting?"

So Crocodile cheered up then, and they painted a simply beautiful picture with yellow and red paint.

A lot of paint went on the floor; and there were red footmarks all round Crocodile's bed. But Sister said she'd never seen such lovely colours mixed together, and put it up on the wall.

CHAPTER THREE

In the morning Nurse Rachel came to take Crocodile down to the X-ray room. Crocodile said he couldn't walk because his legs were too broken, and actually his back felt broken as well. Then he hid under the bedclothes.

"Come on," Nurse Rachel said. "I'll give you a ride in the wheel–chair."

"Can I have my bandages on again if I come?" Crocodile said.

"I'll put them on for you when you're back in bed," Julie said, "and we'll do another painting if you like."

Julie always had her X-ray photographs taken very quickly, because she stood in the right place, held her breath and didn't move. But I'm afraid it took Crocodile a long time.

"Lie there, dear," the X-ray lady said. "Don't move . . . quite still while I count three. One, two . . ."

Crocodile moved his head. "My ear is tickling," he said.

The X-ray lady tried again. "Quite still . . . don't breathe . . . one, two . . ."

Crocodile sneezed twice. "Sorry – it was my nose that time."

"QUITE still! One, two . . ."

"I think I'm going to cough," Crocodile said.

Julie was waiting with the bandages when he got upstairs again. "You were a long time," she said.

"I'm not very good at X-rays, and I've still got a pain. It's my back and my legs. And I can't lift my tail, it feels so heavy."

Nurse Rachel helped Crocodile get into bed.

"You know – your tail looks funny," Julie held out the bandages. "*Very* funny. It's got a bend in the wrong place."

Big tears trickled down Crocodile's nose. "Has it? After – when I fell out of bed, it got shut in the door. It was terrible."

"I'll put a bandage on it then,"

Julie said, and she wound bandages all the way round Crocodile's poor tail.

"Does that feel better?" she said.

"No, but it looks nice."

After dinner Doctor Chumley came back. "Nothing wrong with your X-rays," he said, "how's your pain?"

Crocodile shook his big green head sadly. "Worse," he said. Doctor Chumley looked at him as if he was thinking very hard. "Why have you got a bandage down there – I mean on your tail?"

"It's got a bend in it," Julie said, "quite a bad one. He had an accident, and shut it in the door!"

"I see." Slowly and carefully Doctor Chumley unwrapped the bandage.

"Aha!" he said as he felt crocodile's tail very gently.

"Ouch! OUCH! O U C H !" Crocodile opened his huge mouth full of teeth extremely wide.

"Er – yes." Doctor Chumley moved a little further away. "I should think that's broken alright. Another X-ray, and then we'll have to mend it for you."

"How? How – er – will you mend it?" Crocodile said nervously.

"It won't hurt," Doctor Chumley smiled. "You won't know anything about it. We make you go to sleep first, and then – then we just straighten it; good as new!"

Crocodile thought for a moment, then he began to slide under the bedclothes. "I think I'll have the bandage on again, thank you. It made me feel so much better."

"Don't be silly," Julie said, "that won't mend it. Lie down, and I'll tell you a story about Miss Muffet and the Spider."

"I'm frightened of spiders," Crocodile said, tears coming into his eyes. Julie patted his head.

"Not this spider – it's a specially kind one. Once upon a time . . . there was . . ." Crocodile went to sleep.

CHAPTER FOUR

In the morning Crocodile couldn't have
any breakfast, but Nurse Rachel
brought a beautiful white night gown
and a pair of white woollen socks for
him to put on.

"We want you to look nice and
tidy while you are having your tail
straightened!" She held out the gown and
helped Crocodile put it on.

"It suits you," Julie smiled, "except

the arms are a bit long. Put on your socks. Now you are all ready."

But when the nurses came to take Crocodile to have his poor tail mended, he was nowhere to be seen! Gone! The bed was empty, quite empty. "Oh my goodness! Where is he? That Crocodile, he's gone!"

Nurse Rachel sounded really worried.

Julie began to laugh. "He's in the bathroom looking at himself in his new nightgown," she said, "there's a mirror in there."

"Oh!" Nurse Rachel said, "he is naughty. He shouldn't put his feet on the floor when he's dressed ready to have his tail straightened."

Crocodile was fast asleep on a trolley when he came back with the two nurses. But when they rolled him into bed, Julie was sure his tail was alright again, because it had a beautiful white plaster on it, WITHOUT any bends in the wrong place.

Crocodile woke up when the dinner trolley came in. "Any ice cream?" he said at once. But then he fell asleep; he wasn't really hungry.

The next morning Crocodile was quite his old self again; and he and Julie painted another lovely picture – in red and green and purple. (This time there were green footsteps all around Crocodile's bed.)

Nurse Rachel painted Julie's name in green and purple on Crocodile's plaster.

Crocodile said it tickled, but of course it didn't really.

"How are your – er – broken – legs this morning?" Doctor Chumley asked when he came round to see everyone.

"Better! – well, nearly better. Will you please write your name on my plaster?"

Doctor Chumley laughed, and wrote his name on Crocodile's plaster.

And so did Sister, and Staff Nurse, and Nurse Rachel, and the other nurses, and the Play Lady, and Isabelle, and Alan, and Tony, and John and Jane, and Susan, and Tom and . . . and . . .

Do you know anyone else who wrote their name on that plaster?

Perhaps you did?